T5-CRC-000

NEW HANOVER COUNTY
PUBLIC LIBRARY

DALE EARNHARDT, JR.

JANEY LEVY

HIGH
interest
books

Children's Press®
A Division of Scholastic Inc.
New York / Toronto / London / Auckland / Sydney
Mexico City / New Delhi / Hong Kong
Danbury, Connecticut

Book Design: Michelle Innes
Contributing Editor: Geeta Sobha

Photo Credits: Cover © Chris Stanford/Getty Images; p. 4 © Jamie Squire/Getty Images; p.
8 © Jon Ferrey/Allsport/Getty Images; p. 11 © Jonathan Ferrey/Getty Images; pp. 14–15 ©
Brian Bahr/Getty Images; p. 16 © David Taylor/Getty Images; p. 20 © Craig Jones/Getty
Images; pp. 22–23, 28 © Robert Laberge/Allsport/Getty Images; p. 24 © Chris
Stanford/Allsport/Getty Images; p. 29 © Scott Halleran/Getty Images for NASCAR; p. 30 ©
Rusty Jarrett/Getty Images; pp. 32–33 © Streeter Lecka/Getty Images; p. 35 © Tony
Esparza/CBS Photo Archive/Getty Images; pp. 36–37 © Getty Images; p. 38 © Ezra
Shaw/Getty Images for NASCAR

Library of Congress Cataloging-in-Publication Data

Levy, Janey.
    Dale Earnhardt, Jr. / Janey Levy.
    p. cm. — (Stock car racing)
    Includes index.
    ISBN-10: 0-531-16805-0 (lib. bdg.)   0-531-18713-6 (pbk.)
    ISBN-13: 978-0-531-16805-9 (lib. bdg.) 978-0-531-18713-5 (pbk.)
    1. Earnhardt, Dale, Jr.—Juvenile literature. 2. Automobile racing drivers—
    United States—Biography—Juvenile literature. 3. Stock car racing—United
    States—Juvenile literature. I. Title. II. Series: Stock car racing (Children's
    Press)
    GV1032.E19L49 2007
    796.72092-dc22
    [B]
                                                    2006015131

1 2 3 4 5 6 7 8 9 10 R 11 10 09 08 07

CONTENTS

Dale Earnhardt's Number 8 car pulled ahead of Brian Vickers as they got the green flag.

INTRODUCTION

Almost 200,000 NASCAR fans are on their feet cheering. They have been watching you race—and what a race it has been! There have been twelve cautions. The lead has changed twenty-nine times. Seventeen different drivers have led the race. You've been the leader for almost one-third of the race. That's a great accomplishment for a rookie. Now you are nearly six seconds ahead of the car in second place. That's an incredible lead. The finish line is just ahead. You fly across the finish line—you win the race! This is only your twelfth race in NASCAR's top series. To have won a race so soon is a great achievement. Your team will have a big celebration.

This is the kind of race NASCAR rookies dream about. It does not happen very often, but it happened to one rookie at Texas Motor Speedway in 2000. That rookie was Dale Earnhardt, Jr. He is known by several names. He is called Dale Jr., sometimes simply Junior, or even Little E. Whatever you call him, he's one of the hottest names in NASCAR racing today.

CHAPTER ONE

ALL IN THE FAMILY

Dale Earnhardt, Jr., was born on
October 10, 1974, to Dale Earnhardt,
Sr., and his second wife, Brenda
Gee. Dale Jr. grew up in a racing
family. Dale Earnhardt, Sr.,
won the championship in
NASCAR's top series
seven times. He is
considered one of the
greatest NASCAR
drivers of all time.
Both of Junior's
grandfathers were

also part of NASCAR. Ralph Earnhardt was a champion NASCAR driver. Robert Gee was a mechanic famous for the bodies he made for NASCAR race cars.

Dale Jr. started out racing go-carts. He became more interested in race cars as a teenager. When he was seventeen, he and his older half brother, Kerry, bought an old Chevrolet Monte Carlo. They took turns racing it in the street stock division at the Concord Motorsports Park near their home in North Carolina. Their sister, Kelley, sometimes raced it, too. Dale Sr. encouraged his children's interest in racing.

Soon Dale Jr. became serious about a racing career. He raced in the street stock division for two years, then moved up to NASCAR's late model division. He raced late models from 1994 to 1996 and won three races. He finished in the top five more than half the time and finished in the top ten more than three-quarters of the time!

PAYING HIS WAY

Although Dale Jr. was a professional racer, he could not earn much money from racing at this level. Racing cars is expensive, and since he did not have a sponsor yet,

Junior needed to pay all the costs. His father could afford to pay for Junior's racing, but he did not. Dale Sr. thought that anyone who really wanted to race would find a way to pay for it. He believed the effort and the hard work built character. Dale Jr. had to pay his own way. He worked as a mechanic at his dad's car dealership, where he earned $180 per week.

MOVING ON UP

Dale Jr. eventually decided he wanted to move up to the Busch Series. This series is just one level below

Most people thought that 2000 would be Junior's big year. Dale Sr., however, was the one in the family to finish big. He was second in the points standings for the year.

STAYING IN SCHOOL

Dale Earnhardt, Sr., quit school in the ninth grade to focus on his racing career. He later realized that was a mistake. He did not want his children to make the same mistake, so he always talked to them about the importance of an education. Dale Jr. attended Mitchell Community College in Statesville, North Carolina, and got an automotive degree.

the Nextel Cup, which is NASCAR's top series. Dale Sr. did not think that Junior was ready for the Busch Series. Racing at this level is very expensive. He did not think Dale Jr. could afford it.

Junior did get the funds together, and in June 1996, he drove in his first Busch Series race. It was the Carolina Pride/Red Dog 250 in Myrtle Beach, South Carolina. Dale Jr. finished fourteenth—a great finish for a driver in his first Busch race. He was only twenty-one years old.

The next year Dale Jr. qualified for eight Busch Series races. He did pretty well in these races. He finished seventh in the Detroit Gasket 200 at the Michigan International Speedway—this was his best finish. This showed he was really ready to race at this level. Dale Sr. realized it too. Finally, he was ready to make Junior a business offer.

DRIVING DEI

Dale Sr. and his third wife, Teresa, had formed Dale Earnhardt, Inc. (DEI) in 1980. The company built and sold race cars. It also owned a car that raced in the Busch Series and a truck that raced in NASCAR's Craftsman Truck Series.

In 1998, the driver for the Busch Series car moved up to the Nextel Cup Series, which was then called the Winston Cup Series. DEI needed a new Busch Series driver. Dale Sr. knew just who that should be. He hired Dale Jr. to drive the DEI Busch Series car in 1998. Like

FAST FACT

Dale is Junior's middle name, not his first name. His full name is Ralph Dale Earnhardt, Jr. His dad's full name was Ralph Dale Earnhardt, Sr.

Junior's first car, this car was also a Chevrolet Monte Carlo. Dale Sr.'s decision proved to be a very good one for both DEI and Dale Jr.

Dale Jr. shows off his trophy after winning the Hotwheels.com 300. Dale Sr. (second from left) and Teresa (far left) look on proudly.

CHAPTER TWO

KEEPING TRACK OF JUNIOR

Junior's following years in the Busch Series were successful. The first Busch race of 1998 was the NAPA Auto Parts 300 at the Daytona International Speedway. Dale Jr. started in the third position but crashed during the race and finished thirty-seventh. He did better in the next race. Dale Jr. qualified sixth and finished sixteenth. He won the pole position in the sixth race of the season at Bristol Motor Speedway—and he finished second. The pole is the first starting position for a race. Then he won the seventh race of the season at Texas Motor Speedway.

Dale Jr. went on to win the championship in his first full season in the Busch Series. It was a great achievement, and it earned Dale Jr. financial support for the future. He signed a deal worth $50 million with Budweiser. The beer company would continue to be his sponsor when he moved up to the Winston Cup Series.

Junior's second season in the Busch Series proved to be just as good as his first. In fact, the numbers for his 1999 season were almost identical to those for his 1998 season. Once again, he won three poles. He won six races in 1999. That's more than any other driver in the Busch Series won that year. He had eighteen top-five finishes and twenty-two top-ten finishes—more than any other driver that year. He won the championship again. This made him only the fourth driver in the history of the Busch Series to win the championship two years in a row.

WINSTON CUP

Having Budweiser as his sponsor made it possible for Dale Jr. to launch his Winston Cup career in 1999. The idea was to run a few races to gain experience before moving up to the Winston Cup full time in 2000. Dale Jr. took part in only five Winston Cup races in 1999. He drove DEI's Number 8 Chevrolet Monte Carlo.

On April 2, 2002, Dale Jr. came in fourth at the DirectTV 500 in Martinsville, Virginia.

These races did more than give Dale Jr. the chance to gain valuable experience racing against the best drivers in NASCAR. He also was able to prove that he was talented enough for racing at this level. His first Winston Cup race was at Charlotte Motor Speedway on May 30. Out of forty-three cars in that race, he qualified for the eighth starting position and finished sixteenth. In his next race, he finished last. However, Junior came back strong to finish twenty-fourth in his third race.

THE POLE POSITION

The pole position is the best starting point for a racer. Pole positions are determined by how fast drivers go during qualifying runs. In qualifying, each driver individually runs a few laps around the track as fast as he or she can go. The one who goes the fastest gets to start the race on the front row in the inside spot. This is known as the pole position. The term "pole position" actually carried over to car racing from horse racing.

In his fourth race, he finished tenth out of forty-three cars. That race was at Richmond International Raceway in September. At the Atlanta Motor Speedway in November, he actually led for one lap! That was his last Winston Cup race in 1999. Dale Jr. was clearly ready to move up to the Winston Cup Series full time.

From 1996 to 2006, Dale earned over $41 million in Winston Cup/Nextel Cup and Busch Series races!

CHAPTER THREE

TRIUMPH AND TRAGEDY

Junior's rookie year in the Winston Cup Series was 2000. He had mixed results in his first few races. Dale Jr. finished thirteenth in the first race and nineteenth in the second race. He finished tenth in the third race and even led that race for forty-two laps. The fifth race did not turn out so well. Dale Jr. qualified tenth, but he crashed during the race and finished fortieth. His bad luck continued. He crashed again in the sixth race, held at Bristol Motor Speedway.

SPEED RACER

Junior's seventh race was at Texas Motor Speedway. It proved to be one of the most exciting races ever held at that track. There were twelve cautions, more than in any other Winston Cup race there. The lead changed twenty-nine times. Seventeen different drivers led during the race.

Dale Jr. led 106 laps, far more than any other driver that day. Furthermore, he was leading when it counted most—at the end. He crossed the finish line almost six seconds ahead of the driver in second place. The crowd went wild. Almost 200,000 fans were on their feet cheering. Dale Jr. himself was screaming with joy as he crossed the finish line. It was an incredibly exciting win for a rookie driver. It was only Dale's twelfth Winston Cup race.

A SPECIAL YEAR

Dale Jr. went on to win the sixteenth race of the season. Two weeks later he became the first rookie ever to win the Winston All-Star Race. This race is for winning drivers of the previous and current seasons. Dale Jr. also won two poles in 2000. When the season ended, he was sixteenth overall in points. Drivers earn points in each race based on how well they do in the race. The driver with the most points at the end of the season wins the championship. Finishing sixteenth in the points is very good for a rookie. It helped Dale Jr. become runner-up for the Rookie of the Year title.

In 2000, Dale Jr., Kerry, and Dale Sr. (right) raced against each other at the Pepsi 400—only the second time in NASCAR history that a father raced against his sons.

Dale Jr. had a great rookie year, but 2000 was a special year to him for another reason as well. He and Dale Sr. became close for the first time. They weren't just father and son. They were best friends. A whole new chapter in their relationship was beginning. Junior was beginning to experience what it was like to get unwanted media attention. He began to look to his father for advice and guidance.

TRAGEDY

At the Daytona 500, the first race of the season, things were looking good. Three DEI drivers—Dale Jr., Michael Waltrip, and Dale Sr.—were running at the front near the end of the race. It looked like the three of them might finish first, second, and third. Many people think that Dale Sr. was actually trying to block the drivers behind the trio from taking over the lead. Then, on the last lap, Dale Sr. crashed into the wall. This one seemed no different from many other crashes. The race continued.

Michael went on to win. Dale Jr. came in second. It was an exciting moment for both drivers. Then they got the terrible news. Dale Sr. had been killed in the crash. Dale Jr. had lost his dad, his boss, and his best friend all at once.

RACING IN DAD'S HONOR

Dale Jr. went to the race the next weekend at North Carolina Speedway. He—and all the other drivers—felt like they had to keep racing. That was their way of dealing with the tragedy. Dale Jr. was not ready to race again, however. He crashed into the wall on the first lap of the race. Fortunately, Dale Jr. received only minor injuries and was able to walk away from the crash.

In July, Dale Jr. took part in a race at Daytona International Speedway. Going back to the racetrack where his father had been killed was very hard for

him. Still, he led the race for 116 laps and won the race! It was a very emotional moment—everyone could not help but think of Dale Sr. The fans went

Above: Fans wave flags in honor of Dale Sr. at the North Carolina Speedway on February 26, 2001.

Left: Vehicles removing Dale Sr.'s car from the scene of his fatal accident.

Sponsors pay NASCAR race teams to advertise their products with, for example, company logos on the race cars.

wild. Other drivers jumped out of their cars and rushed to congratulate Junior. He announced that he dedicated his victory to his dad. It seemed to be the perfect way to honor his father's memory.

Dale Jr. had a good year on the racetrack in 2001. After his win at Daytona, he went on to win two more races. He also won two poles. Altogether, he had nine top-five finishes and fifteen top-ten finishes. He finished the season eighth in points. Would the future be as bright for Dale Jr. without his dad?

FAST FACT

When Dale Jr. won the 1998 Busch series championship, there were three generations of NASCAR champions in his family. That was the first time that had ever happened in NASCAR history.

CHAPTER FOUR

CHASING A CHAMPIONSHIP

As the 2002 season started, Dale Jr. seemed more mature and committed to racing. He had new responsibilities. With his dad gone, he played a more important role at DEI. He also wanted to become the best driver he could be, winning races and championships. He still had not won the championship in NASCAR's top series, but he was now determined to do so.

In April, Dale Jr. suffered a concussion in a race accident and did not do well in several races after that. His performance eventually improved though. He won two poles and two races in 2002. He also had eleven top-five finishes and sixteen top-ten finishes. He finished the season eleventh in points.

DALE'S QUEST

The next year, 2003, was Dale's best in the Winston Cup Series. He won two races and had thirteen top-five finishes and twenty-one top-ten finishes. He ranked third in points at the end of the season.

In 2004, the Winston Cup Series became the Nextel Cup Series. Dale's racing career was only getting better. He won six races, the most he had ever won in a single season. One of those was the Daytona 500, the biggest race in NASCAR. Altogether, Dale Jr. had sixteen top-five finishes and twenty-one top-ten finishes. He finished the season fifth in points.

Personal problems began to affect Dale Jr. in 2005. He was not getting along with his cousin Tony Eury, Jr., who was his car chief. By the end of the season, the two were not speaking to each other. DEI decided that a change was needed. Eury switched places with another car chief for the 2005 season.

This change in crews helped Junior's relationship with his cousin, but it did not help his racing. Dale Jr. had his worst year ever in 2005. He won only one race. He managed to get seven top-five finishes and thirteen top-ten finishes. By the end of the season, though, he was nineteenth in points. That was his lowest ranking ever.

Here, Dale Jr. and his team celebrate their victory after winning the Daytona 500 in February 2004.

MEET THE BOSS

Junior's racing career goes beyond his role as a driver. He is also a team owner. Since 2002, he has owned Chance 2 Motorsports with his stepmother, Teresa. He has two championships as team owner. Driver Martin Truex, Jr., won Busch Series championships for Chance 2 Motorsports in 2004 and 2005. In addition to Chance 2 Motorsports, Dale Jr. owns JR Motorsports. This company started out running cars in the street stock series. Beginning in 2006, it also runs a car in the Busch Series.

Tony Eury (left) worked with Dale Sr., winning races in the Busch Series. Today, he continues his work, successfully leading Dale Jr. (right) to many victories.

Budweiser

Dale Jr. decided to work out his differences with Eury. Eury went back to work with Dale Jr. as his crew chief for the last ten races of the 2005 season. That led many people to think that Dale Jr. would have a great year in 2006 since he was working with his cousin again. Dale Jr. himself predicted that he would win six or seven races before the Chase for the Nextel Cup at the end of the season. The Chase is NASCAR's version of a play-off series. Perhaps 2006 will be the year Dale Jr. finally wins the Nextel Cup championship. Winning the championship might make Dale Jr. even more popular and busier than he already is—if that's possible.

A POPULAR DRIVER

Dale Jr. has been a popular driver since the early days of his Busch Series career. In those days, he signed autographs for fans before races. These meetings with fans were supposed to last

FAST FACT

Dale Jr. hopes one day to drive the Number 3 car that his dad drove. He thinks it would be a great way to end his Nextel Cup career.

half an hour, but often lasted longer. Once, he even had to be "rescued" by his crew or he would have been late for the start of the race!

He has gained more fans since he moved to NASCAR's top series. Dale Jr. has helped make stock car racing popular and has drawn new fans to the sport. Fans voted him NASCAR's Most Popular Driver three years in a row—2003, 2004, and 2005. Dale Jr. feels it is a great honor to win this award. He said it was even more special in 2005, when he had his worst year. Having so much fan support during a difficult year meant a lot to him.

OFF TRACK

Dale Jr. is also a celebrity outside of the world of stock car racing. Much has been written about him, from books to magazine articles. He has been listed as one of *Forbes* magazine's "Top 100 Celebrities" and has been on more than ninety magazine covers. He is the only NASCAR driver ever to have been the subject of a story in *Rolling Stone*.

Sportscasts are not the only spots on radio and television to catch Dale Jr. This NASCAR racer has been a guest on numerous television talk shows. In 2006,

Pushing ahead, Dale Jr. won the Crown Royal 400 in May 2006.

Dale Jr. hosted a television series about the early days of NASCAR called *Back in the Day*. He hosts a weekly satellite radio show, where he discusses NASCAR, music, video games, and many other subjects.

Dale Jr. has been the subject of programs on MTV and VH-1. He has also appeared in music videos by artists such as Sheryl Crow, Three Doors Down, the Matthew Good Band, and Trace Adkins. Dale Jr. even had small parts in two 2006 movies—an animated film titled *Cars* and a comedy about NASCAR starring Will Ferrell.

SHARING HIS FORTUNE

Dale Jr. knows he is fortunate to be able to do something he loves and to earn a good living doing it. He feels it is important to give something back, so he gives generously to a number of charities. Dale Jr.

FAST FACT

Sponsors know that they can bank on Dale's popularity. He appears in ads for sponsors such as Budweiser, Nextel, Wrangler, NAPA, and Gillette.

Here, Dale appears at a fund-raising event for the New York Police and Firefighters Widows and Children's Benefit Fund.

sponsors the Dale Jr. Celebrity Sports Auction to benefit the Make-A-Wish Foundation of Central and Western North Carolina.

He also makes donations to a long list of other charities. Not surprisingly, one of these is the Dale Earnhardt Foundation. This foundation was created

after Dale Sr.'s death to provide grants for causes that were important to Dale Sr. These causes include education, children, and the environment. Supporting the Dale Earnhardt Foundation also gives Dale Jr. another way to honor his father's memory.

In August 2002, Dale Earnhardt's pit crew took part in the Drakkar Noir Pit Crew Challenge, a charity race to perform pit crew duties.

So what's next for Dale Jr.? He and his thousands of fans certainly hope it includes at least one Nextel Cup championship. And who knows where his

television and radio shows might take him? So stay tuned and keep watching. This NASCAR superstar is still on the rise!

Here's Dale in a familiar position—at the head of the pack at the Sharpie 500 in Bristol, Tennessee.

DALE EARNHARDT, JR. TIMELINE

October 10, 1974	Born in Kannapolis, North Carolina, to NASCAR racer Dale Earnhardt and his wife, Brenda
1992	Begins racing in street stock division at Concord Motorsports Park
1994	Begins racing late model cars
June 22, 1996	Runs first Busch Series race, the Carolina Pride/Red Dog 250 at Myrtle Beach Speedway
1997	Runs eight Busch Series races; best finish is seventh, in the Detroit Gasket 200 at Michigan International Speedway
1998	First full year in Busch Series; wins championship; signs sponsorship deal worth $50 million with Budweiser

DALE EARNHARDT, JR. TIMELINE

1999	Wins Busch Series championship again; runs five races in Winston Cup Series
2000	Rookie year in Winston Cup Series
2001	Comes in second at Daytona 500, the race in which his father has a fatal crash; Dale Jr. wins Pepsi 400 at Daytona
2002	Wins two races; becomes co-owner of Chance 2 Motorsports
2003	Wins two races; wins Most Popular Driver award
2004	Wins Daytona 500; wins a total of six races; wins Most Popular Driver award
2005	Wins only one race; wins Most Popular Driver award

NEW WORDS

achievement (uh-**cheev**-munht) something done successfully, especially after a great effort

caution (**kaw**-shun) in racing, a period following an accident when racers have to drive more slowly and no passing is allowed

celebrity (suh-**leb**-ruh-tee) a famous person

concussion (kuhn-**kush**-uhn) an injury to the brain caused by a heavy blow to the head

congratulate (kuhn-**grach**-uh-late) to tell someone that you are pleased because something good has happened or he or she has done something well

crew chief (**kru cheef**) the person in charge of the crew of people who work on a race car in the garage

donations (**doh**-nay-shunz) things given as gifts, especially to a charity

green flag (**green flag**) this flag is used to signal the start of a race

NEW WORDS

mechanic (muh-kan-ik) someone who is skilled at operating or repairing machinery

predicted (pri-dikt-uhd) to have said what will happen in the future

racetrack (rayss-trak) a round or oval course that is used for racing

rookie (ruk-ee) someone who is in their first season in a major professional sport

speedway (speed-way) a racetrack for cars

sponsor (spon-sur) a company that gives money to a race team and driver in exchange for the right to place advertising on the car and team uniforms; a sponsor also gets to use the driver and the car in advertisements

stock car (stok kar) a race car built to look like an ordinary car

tragedy (traj-uh-dee) a very sad event

FOR FURTHER READING

Buckley, James. *NASCAR*. New York: DK Children's
  Publishing, 2005.

Cavin, Curt. *Under the Helmet: Inside the Mind of a Driver*.
  Chanhassen, MN: Child's World, 2003.

Gigliotti, Jim. *Dale Earnhardt, Jr.: Tragedy and Triumph*.
  Farmington Hills, MI: Tradition Publishing, 2004.

Kelley, K. C., and Bob Woods. *Young Stars of NASCAR*.
  Pleasantville, NY: Reader's Digest Children's
  Publishing, 2005.

Schaefer, A. R. *Dale Earnhardt Jr*. Mankato, MN: Capstone
  Press, 2005.

Stewart, Mark. *Dale Earnhardt Jr.: Driven by Destiny*.
  Brookfield, CT: The Millbrook Press, Inc., 2003.

Woods, Bob. *Earning a Ride: How to Become a NASCAR
  Driver*. Chanhassen, MN: Child's World, 2003.

RESOURCES

ORGANIZATIONS

American Speed Association (ASA) Racing
457 South Ridgewood Ave., Suite 101
Daytona Beach, FL 32114
(386) 258-2221
www.asa-racing.com

National Association for Stock Car Auto Racing
(NASCAR)
1801 W. International Speedway Blvd.
Daytona Beach, FL 32115
(386) 253-0611
www.nascar.com

USAC National Office
4910 W. 16th St.
Speedway, IN 46224
(317) 247-5151
www.usacracing.com

RESOURCES

WEB SITES

Dale Earnhardt Inc.
www.daleearnhardtinc.com
This site has everything you need to know about DEI and the Earnhardt family.

JR Motorsports
www.jrmotorsport.com
Check out this site for the latest information on Junior's racing company.

NASCAR
www.nascar.com
Log on to NASCAR's official Web site to find out how Junior did on his latest race.

The Official Site of Dale Earnhardt Jr.
www.dalejr.com
This is Junior's official Web site. Click on the fan garage link to see photos and videos or listen to Junior on the radio.

INDEX

ABOUT THE AUTHOR
Janey Levy is a writer and editor who lives in Colden,
New York. She is the author of more than fifty books for
young people.